KNOW

"Dogs think they are human, cats ~~think~~ they are gods."

— Anonymous

For Edgar — J.F.F.

Dedicated to Martin who has been my support and rock,
and loves cats almost as much as I do — A.K.

ACKNOWLEDGMENTS

Special thanks to Professor Joshua J. Mark for sharing his knowledge of Pelusium and the process of
piecing together history, from ancient battles to Led Zeppelin concerts.

Text © 2024 Jenny Fox
Illustrations © 2024 Anna Kwan

Published in Canada and the U.S. by Kids Can Press Ltd.
25 Dockside Drive, Toronto, ON M5A 0B5

Kids Can Press is a Corus Entertainment Inc. company

www.kidscanpress.com

The artwork in this book was drawn in ink and colored digitally in Photoshop.
The text is set in Supernett.

Edited by Patricia Ocampo
Designed by Andrew Dupuis

Printed and bound in Dongguan, Guangdong, P.R. China in 3/2024 by Toppan Leefung

CM 24 0 9 8 7 6 5 4 3 2 1

FSC
www.fsc.org
MIX
Paper | Supporting
responsible forestry
FSC® C104723

LIBRARY AND ARCHIVES CANADA CATALOGUING IN PUBLICATION

Title: The pharaoh vs. the felines / J. F. Fox; [illustrated by] Anna Kwan.
Other titles: Pharaoh versus the felines
Names: Fox, Jennifer, 1976– author. | Kwan, Anna, 1991– illustrator.
Description: Includes bibliographical references.
Identifiers: Canadiana (print) 20230568289 | Canadiana (ebook) 20230568297
| ISBN 9781525306525 (hardcover) | ISBN 9781525308147 (EPUB)
Subjects: LCSH: Amasis II, King of Egypt — Juvenile literature. | LCSH: Cambyses II, King of Persia, -522 B.C. — Juvenile literature.
| LCSH: Animals — War use — Egypt — History — To 332 B.C. — Juvenile literature. | LCSH: Pelusium (Extinct city) — History,
Military — Juvenile literature. | LCSH: Egypt — History, Military — Juvenile literature. | LCSH: Egypt — History — To 332 B.C. —
Juvenile literature. | LCGFT: Informational works.
Classification: LCC DT90 .F69 2024 | DDC j932/.015 — dc23

Kids Can Press gratefully acknowledges that the land on which our office is located is the traditional territory of many nations,
including the Mississaugas of the Credit, the Anishnabeg, the Chippewa, the Haudenosaunee and the Wendat peoples, and is now
home to many diverse First Nations, Inuit and Métis peoples.

We thank the Government of Ontario, through Ontario Creates and the Ontario Arts Council; the Canada Council for the Arts; and the
Government of Canada for their financial support of our publishing activity.

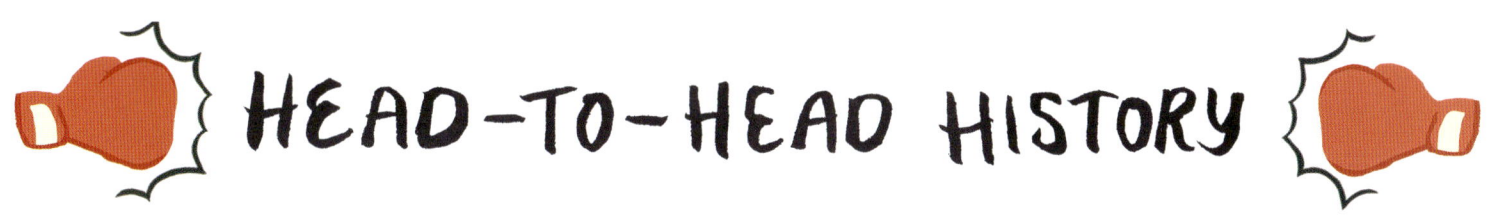

HEAD-TO-HEAD HISTORY

THE
PHARAOH
VS.
THE
FELINES

J. F. Fox
Anna Kwan

Kids Can Press

Ancient Egypt was one of the world's first empires.

Nestled on the banks of the Nile River, it was a place of culture, invention and curiosity, ruled for centuries by powerful kings, known later as pharaohs, with powerful armies. Nothing, it seemed, could threaten their greatness.

That is, until one particular rival came up with a CATastrophic
plan that would change the course of Egyptian *hiss*-tory.

Before we find out what happened with the
cats, let's slink on back to where it all started.

This curve of land spanned multiple countries in what is now called the Middle East.

It was known for its rich soil and ample grain crops, which could feed many.

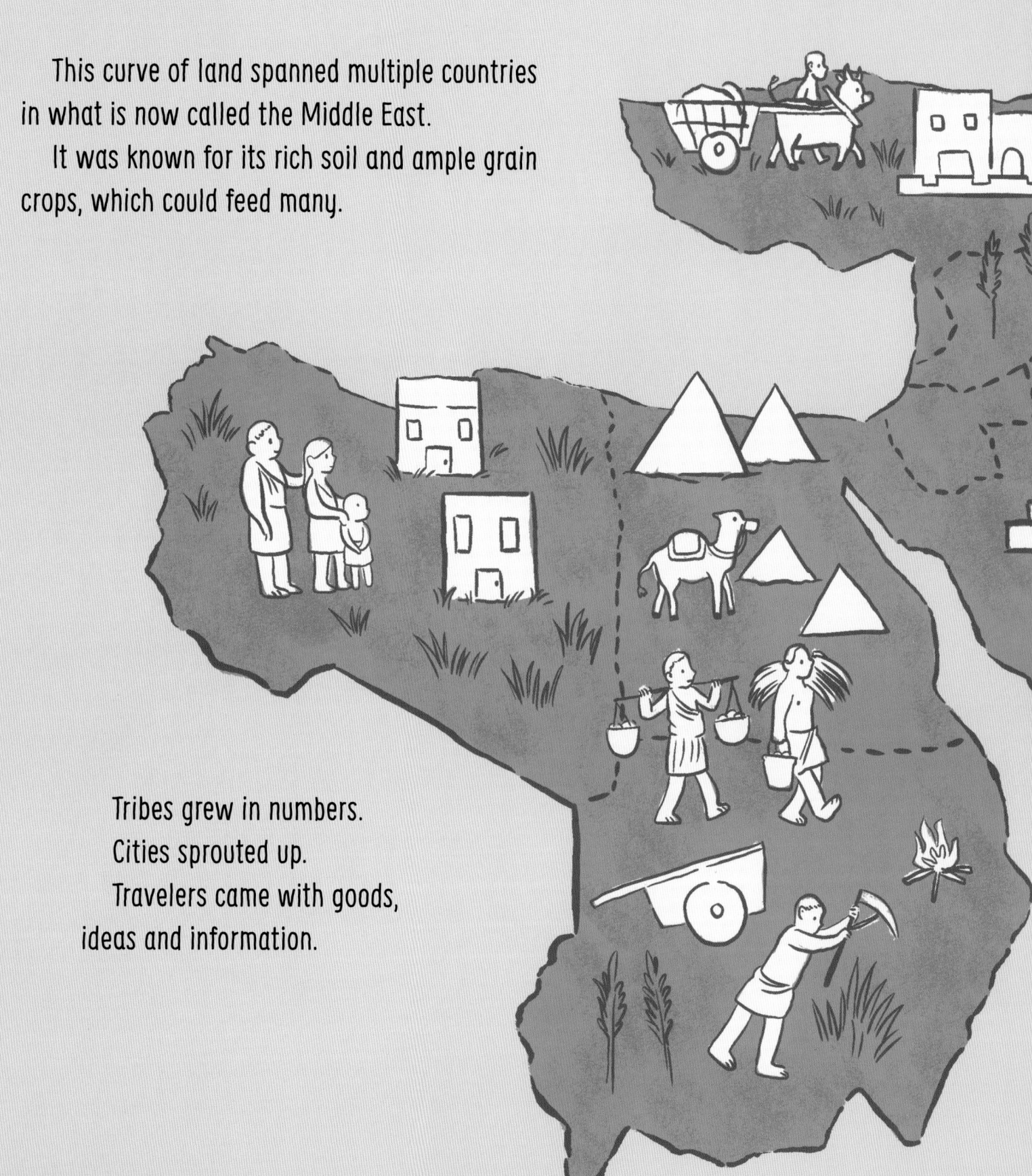

Tribes grew in numbers.
Cities sprouted up.
Travelers came with goods,
ideas and information.

Writing, science, religion and farming flourished — as did inventions, such as the wheel.

AND BEER.
HICCUP

Trouble also brewed here.

Two great powers, Egypt and Persia, both wanted control of this important area.

For years, there were squabbles and struggles.

And then, it all boiled over.

What finally brought the trouble to a bubble?

In this case, the person who got tricked was Cambyses II, the ruler of Persia.

Cambyses had asked to marry the daughter of Pharaoh Amasis II, the ruler of Egypt. Cambyses knew his request would put Amasis in a tight spot.

And it did! You see, Amasis did not want to send his daughter off to a different country.

Egyptians believed anyone who died outside of Egypt could be lost in the afterlife.

On the other hand, if he *didn't* say yes, Cambyses might take it as an insult — maybe even start a war.

Amasis needed a clever idea to get out of this bind —
and he thought he had one.

The pharaoh found a different young woman, dressed
her up as royalty and sent *her* off to Persia to pretend to
be the princess.

Great idea, right?

WRONG!

When the young woman reached Persia, she confessed that she was *not*, in fact, the daughter of the pharaoh.

YEAH, NOPE.

Cambyses was NOT happy. So he decided to invade Egypt.

But Egypt had a mighty army. Cambyses needed to be sure Persia would win. He asked his advisors to tell him everything they knew about Egypt.

Cambyses paced and pondered.
Then, he got a clever idea.

Yes, Egyptians were feline fanatics. But why?

Ancient Egyptians were a farming people. They lived closely with nature.

Poisonous snakes were a daily danger.

Rats and mice carried diseases and germs and ate up crops,
such as wheat, that the Egyptians needed for food.

Cats hunted these pests and became cherished pets,
protecting the health and homes of Egyptian families.

Cats were so important to their way of life that the Egyptians began to worship a cat goddess named Bastet. She kept families safe both on Earth and in the afterlife.

Yes, Ancient Egypt was a completely cat-crazy culture.
And that is the very thing Cambyses decided to use against them.

In 525 BCE, Cambyses and his army were ready to invade Egypt.

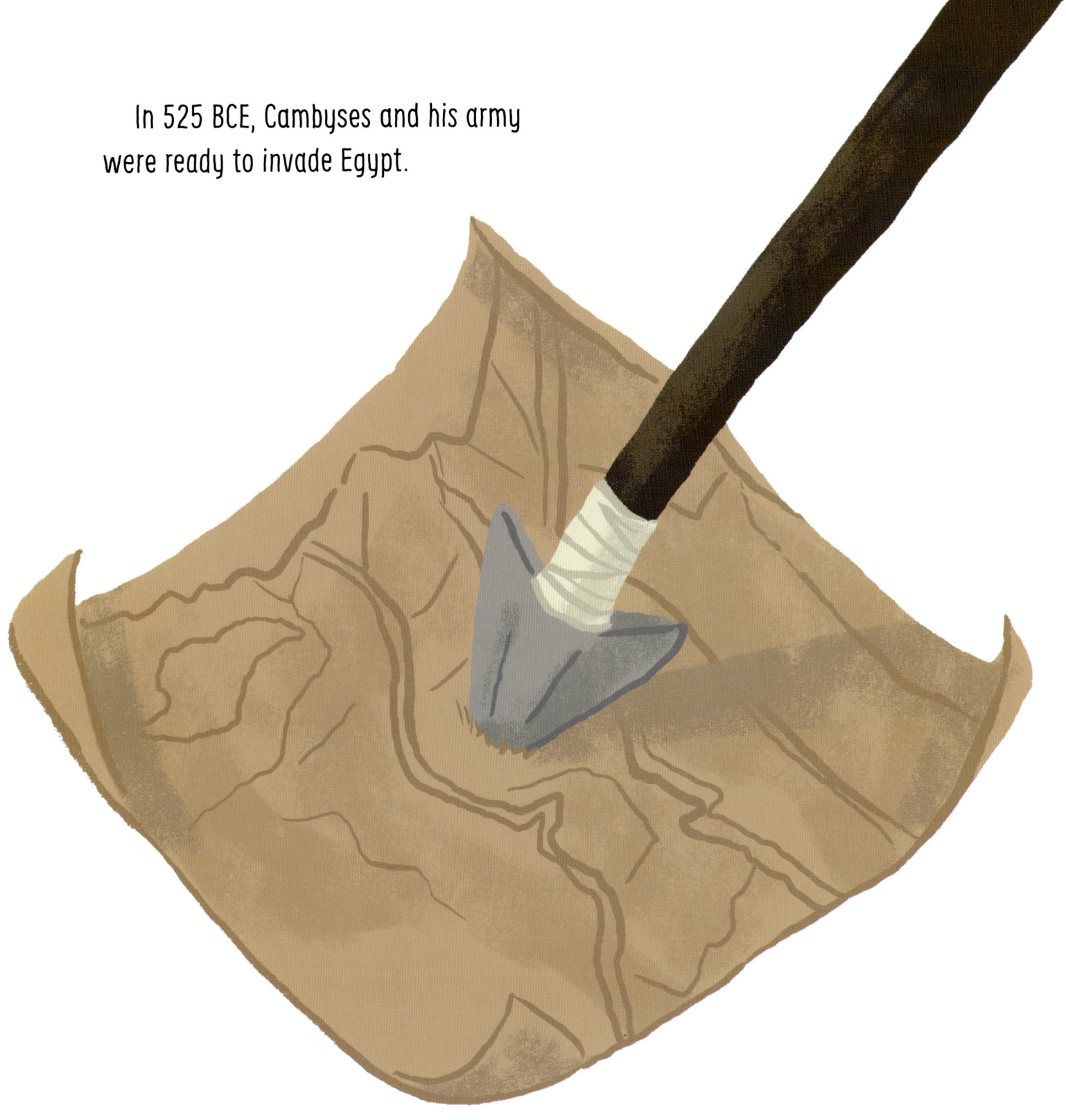

For his point of attack, Cambyses chose Pelusium, a key city that sat where Africa met Asia and the Nile River flowed into the Mediterranean Sea.

It's true. The great Amasis, who had ruled Egypt for more than forty years, died about six months before the battle.

Now his inexperienced son, Psamtik III, was pharaoh —
and he was facing down a massive war.

GULP

As the story goes, on that fateful day in 525, Cambyses and his men marched into Pelusium.

They were armed not just with weapons but with Cambyses's very clever battle-winning idea — CATS!

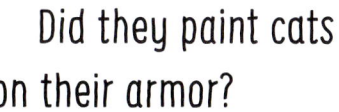

Did they paint cats
on their armor?

Or position the creatures
kitty-corner to their enemy?

Or — Ra forbid —
use a cat-a-pult?!

However they did it, it worked. Facing felines on the frontlines, the pharaoh's army would not fight and risk harming the cherished creatures. Cambyses conquered those cat-lovers.

I guess you could say, that day on the battlefield, brains triumphed over brawn.

Cambyses became the new ruler of Egypt
and was never catfished again!

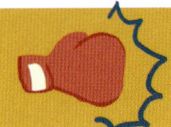

MYSTERY vs. HISTORY

Around 3000 BCE	Around 1500 BCE	570 BCE	Around 529 BCE	526 BCE	525 BCE	525 to about 331 BCE	1 CE	2024 CE
Bastet is first worshipped as a lioness goddess	Bastet takes on the form of a house cat	Amasis II becomes pharaoh	Cambyses II begins reign as king of Persia	Amasis II dies; Psamtik III becomes pharaoh	Cambyses II invades Egypt at the Battle of Pelusium	Egypt under Persian rule for almost 200 years		(contemporary time)

The Battle of Pelusium showed just how serious the ancient Egyptians were about their cats and their gods and goddesses. This was not a fight they would have taken lightly, and the consequences of the loss were severe. After the battle, Persia would go on to rule Egypt for almost 200 years.

How do we even know about things that happened so long ago? As any scholar will tell you, figuring out history can be a little im-*purr*-fect, and the further back you go, the more puzzling things can be.

Let's take a look at some ways history can be confused and clarified.

CONFUSED

- *Points of view* — No two people remember something in the exact same way.
- *Scarce sources* — Long ago there were no computers, cameras, newspapers or even notebooks.
- *The telephone game* — Over time, stories and details can change with retelling.

CLARIFIED

- *Eyewitnesses* — Firsthand reports from a person, or better yet, *people* who were there.
- *Context* — What else do we know about the period and what life was like that would support a certain scenario?
- *Consistency* — When multiple reliable sources tell essentially the same story it is more likely to be true.

THE BATTLE OF PELUSIUM — CONFUSED

- It happened thousands of years ago and anyone who witnessed it is long gone.
- Few written accounts of the battle from the ancient point of view exist.
- The story has been passed down by word of mouth for thousands of years, and accounts sometimes differ in the details.

THE BATTLE OF PELUSIUM — CLARIFIED

- Based on stories from the time — passed down orally and later written down — Cambyses II was known to be an ambitious and ruthless ruler.
- We know the ancient Egyptians deeply revered cats and worshipped cat-like gods, and that anyone who killed a cat in ancient Egypt could be given a death sentence. This supports the idea that the Egyptians would not risk hurting cats.
- A couple of ancient historians *did* write about the battle (after the time in which it happened). Herodotus, known by many as the world's first historian, mentioned the battle and its outcome. Polyaenus, who wrote about war strategies, specifically mentioned Cambyses using sacred animals, such as cats, on his front line (as defense).

GLOSSARY

afterlives/afterlife: a spiritual life after the death of the physical body on Earth

brawn: strength or might

cartouche: a framed set of Egyptian hieroglyphs, often representing a pharaoh, similar to a coat of arms

catapult: an ancient weapon that used a lever with a bucket (often on a wheeled cart) to fling large stones, flaming objects or sharpened wood

catastrophic: terrible, destructive, causing a very bad outcome

catfishing: tricking someone into believing you are someone else, most often on the computer or internet

Fertile Crescent: a banana-shaped region in the Middle East, where many ancient civilizations sprang up due to the rich soil, which produced abundant crops

kitty-corner: diagonally opposite (also known as catty-corner)

papyrus: thick paper made from the stems of a reedy water plant

pharaoh: ruler in ancient Egypt; the word originally meant "great house" or palace

Ra: the sun god, considered the greatest or king of the Egyptian gods

scarab: a beetle frequently seen in Egyptian hieroglyphs, art and jewelry

scribe: someone (usually a man) who could read and write and served as a notetaker or historian

squabbles: small fights or arguments

SOURCES

PRINT

David, Rosalie. *Religion and Magic in Ancient Egypt*. London: Penguin Books, 2002.

Herodotus. *Herodotus: The Histories*. Translation by Robin Waterfield. Oxford: Oxford University Press, 2008.

Jackson, Lesley. *Sekhmet & Bastet: The Feline Powers of Egypt*. London: Avalonia, 2020.

Málek, Jaromír. *The Cat in Ancient Egypt*. Philadelphia: University of Pennsylvania Press, 2019.

Pinch, Geraldine. *Egyptian Mythology: A Guide to the Gods, Goddesses, and Traditions of Ancient Egypt*. Oxford: Oxford University Press, 2004.

Polyaenus (of Lampsacus). *Polyaenus's Stratagems of War*. Translation by R. Shepherd, F.R.S. London: George Nicol, 1793.

Wilkinson, Richard H. *The Complete Gods and Goddesses of Ancient Egypt*. London: Thames & Hudson, 2003.

DIGITAL

Grimm, David. "Ancient Egyptians May Have Given Cats the Personality to Conquer the World." Science.org. June 19, 2017. https://www.science.org/content/article/ancient-egyptians-may-have-given-cats-personality-conquer-world.

Mark, Joshua J. "Bastet." World History Encyclopedia. July 24, 2016. https://www.worldhistory.org/Bastet/.

Mark, Joshua J. "The Battle of Pelusium: A Victory Decided by Cats." World History Encyclopedia. June 13, 2017. https://www.worldhistory.org/article/43/the-battle-of-pelusium-a-victory-decided-by-cats/.